SPOOKY
and the Bad Luck Raven

By Natalie Savage Carlson · Illustrated by Andrew Glass

Lothrop, Lee & Shepard Books   New York

For Kaitlyn Idell,
Sara Rondolino's little sister
N.S.C.

For Ellen and Shannon and Alexandra Hall
A.G.

Text copyright © 1988 by Natalie Savage Carlson
Illustrations copyright © 1988 by Andrew Glass

Inquiries should be addressed to Lothrop, Lee & Shepard Books, a division of William Morrow & Company, Inc., 105 Madison Avenue, New York, New York 10016. Printed in the United States of America.

First Edition 1 2 3 4 5 6 7 8 9 10

Library of Congress Cataloging-in-Publication Data
Carlson, Natalie Savage. Spooky and the bad luck raven / by Natalie Savage Carlson; illustrated by Andrew Glass.
p.   cm.   Summary: Cats Spooky and Snowball sabotage the Witches' Sabbat Race, creating chaos never before seen at the event. ISBN 0-688-07650-5.   ISBN 0-688-07651-3 (lib. bdg.) [1. Witches—Fiction.   2. Cats—Fiction.]
I. Glass, Andrew, Ill.   II. Title.   PZ7.C2167Sos 1988   [E]—dc19   87-15471. CIP. AC.

The Bascombs had a big black cat with green eyes named Spooky. And they had a little white cat named Snowball. Spooky and Snowball had once belonged to the witch who lived in the woods down the road.

When the moon was ripe, Spooky and Snowball liked to sit on the back fence and watch the night together. But one night Snowball was nowhere to be found. Where was she? Spooky waited and watched the night, but Snowball did not appear.

The next night Spooky jumped up on the back fence. He waited for the little white cat to come back from here or there or somewhere. But she didn't.

Instead, a big black raven came along on flippy, flappy wings and joined Spooky on the fence. It clapped its wings. It croaked dismally. *Crawk, crawk!*

Spooky knew the raven meant bad luck. Could the witch have sent it to let him know that she had Snowball back?

The raven croaked to Spooky again. *Crawk, crawk.* It flapped its black wings. The raven started off, hippety-hop and flutter, through the woods. Spooky followed creepy, crawly.

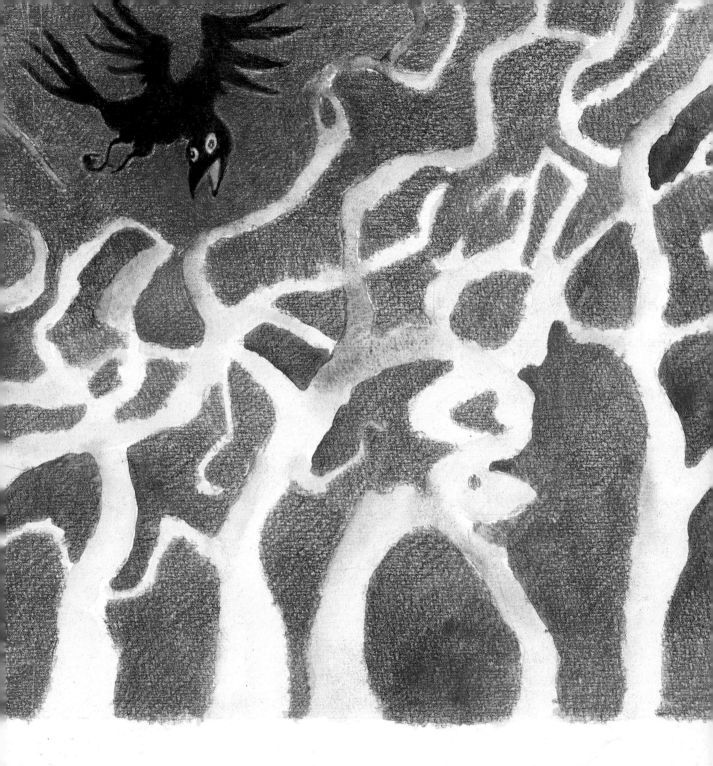

Soon Spooky heard gabble and cackle. The sounds came from a grove of dead trees. In the moonlight the trees stood like skeletons with crooked limbs.

Spooky jumped down from the fence and went pussyfoot, pussyfoot down the road to the woods where the witch lived in a hut under the witch hazel tree. The raven flapped and fluttered behind him. *Crawk, crawk!*

The door of the witch's hut was open. All was dark inside. The witch wasn't home.

Among the trees was a coven of witches. Their brooms were set against the twisted trunks of the trees, and they were gathered in a circle, chanting charms and speaking spells.

Spooky saw Snowball. She was held by the sister of the witch who had once owned them both.

While Spooky tried to figure out how to rescue Snowball, the raven perched on a bony branch above Spooky's head and began to croak loudly. *Crawk, crawk!* The raven pointed its beak down at Spooky.

One of the witches broke away from the circle. She rushed to Spooky. She grabbed him by the nape and shook him like a fur muff.

"So, my little pet, you're back!" the witch cackled. "You must ride with me in the Witches' Sabbat Race."

All the witches grabbed their brooms and lined up for the race. Spooky's witch set him behind her on her broom. And the sister witch set Snowball behind her on *her* broom.

Spooky's witch ordered the raven, "Fly behind us and keep an eye on this cat. Don't let him pull any tricks."

Then she gave the signal, "Flip, flop, flap, FLY!"

They were off with a swish and a swoop. The raven flip-flapped behind Spooky. They flew over the tree skeletons. They flew over the clouds. They flew between the stars. The race stirred up windstorms and cyclones on the earth below.

Spooky's witch was winning, but her sister was closing in. Soon the two sisters were racing, pointy nose to pointy nose. Then Spooky had an idea.

He jumped up and down, and the broom bounced up and down. Spooky bounced the broom so hard, his witch was shaken loose. She turned a somersault in the air and landed on top of her sister with a THUD.

Both witches fell screaming through the air.

Spooky leapt a big leap to Snowball's broom and landed in front of her.

The brooms of all the witches were bumping into one another all around them. *Bump! Crash! Crack!* Broken brooms and spilled witches fell through the air. It was the worst wreck in the history of the Sabbat Races. The raven was caught in the midst of it all, and black feathers flew in every direction.

The sharp claws of the two cats kept them safely on their broom. Spooky turned away from the crackup, and flew the broom back to the empty hut under the witch hazel tree. The cats jumped off and began digging a long deep trench.

The dirt flew. *Flitch, flitch!* Spooky and Snowball dragged the broom over and dropped it in. Then they scratched dirt over it. More *flitch, flitch!*

On the way home through the woods, Spooky and Snowball saw the two witches slowly hobbling along through the trees on crutches of broken broomsticks. Behind them shuffled a bird that looked as if it had been plucked for the stewpot.

When Spooky and Snowball reached the Bascomb house, they jumped up on the fence and once again watched the night together.

They watched the fireflies turning their little lights on and off.

They watched a toad hippety-hop over the grass and snap up a moth.

They watched a garter snake slink and slither through the grass, this way and that way and any way.

Then they watched the Bascomb boy and girl come out with a flashlight to see if Snowball had come back. The Bascomb girl swept the beam of light back and forth over the ground. Then she stooped and picked something up.

"A black feather!" she exclaimed. "I wonder where it came from."

"And here's another," said the Bascomb boy. "That strong wind must have blown the feathers off a crow."

The Bascomb girl raised the light to the fence.
"And there's Snowball back with Spooky," she cried.
"I wonder where she's been."

Spooky and Snowball jumped down from the fence.
They ran to the Bascomb boy and girl. They meowed
the news that they had won the Witches' Sabbat Race.

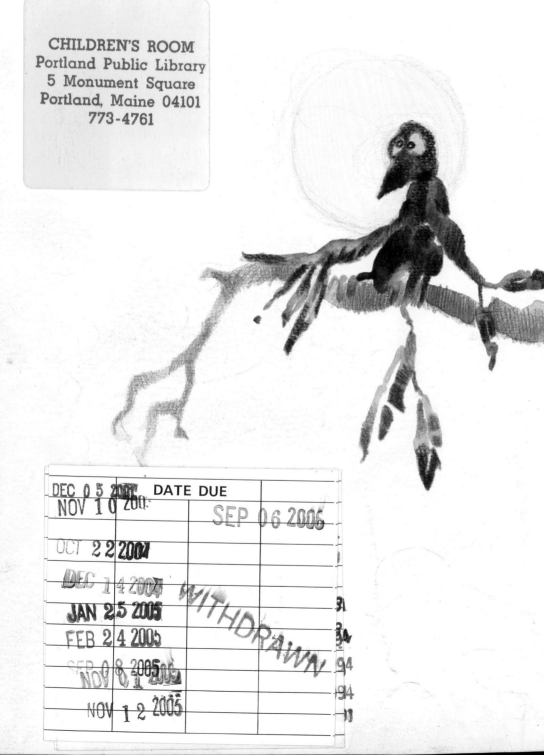